THE ADVENTURES

Christabel
Crocodile

HELGA KNÜPPEL

Magi Publications, London

Published in 1990 by Magi Publications,
in association with Star Books International, 55 Crowland Avenue, Hayes, Middx UB3 4JP.

Printed and bound in Hong Kong.

ISBN 1 85430 189 6

Sunday morning in the zoo.
Mummy wanted to sleep.
Daddy wanted to sleep.
But Christabel wanted to play.

She tickled Mummy.
She jumped on Daddy.
They didn't think it was very funny.

So Christabel went exploring in the pool instead.
She found an old chain and swung on it.
She pulled it very hard and there was a peculiar noise.
It sounded just like a plug popping out.

The water whirled round and round, and Christabel whirled with it.
The more she tried to stop, the more she couldn't.
"Help!" she gurgled.

Down and down went Christabel, swirling and sliding –
anticlockwise.
"If I were in Australia, I would be turning clockwise," she thought.
This wasn't much help, though.

As Christabel was swept along, a rusty old pipe hit her in the tummy. She dangled in mid-air over a dark underground river. She was very scared. She watched the rubbish floating by and wondered how she would ever escape.

"Why don't you jump into that passing box?" suggested a helpful spider. "You can pretend it's a boat."
"Good idea," said Christabel, "but there aren't any paddles."

Away bobbed the boat, carrying Christabel down the swiftly flowing river. Then she saw a rope dangling down from the roof of the tunnel and caught hold of it.

"Ow," said the rope.

"Ropes can't talk," said Christabel holding on tight.

"I'm not a rope," said the rope. "I'm René Rat, and you're holding onto my tail, silly."
The box boat rocked and bucked, and tipped them both out, and then sailed away.

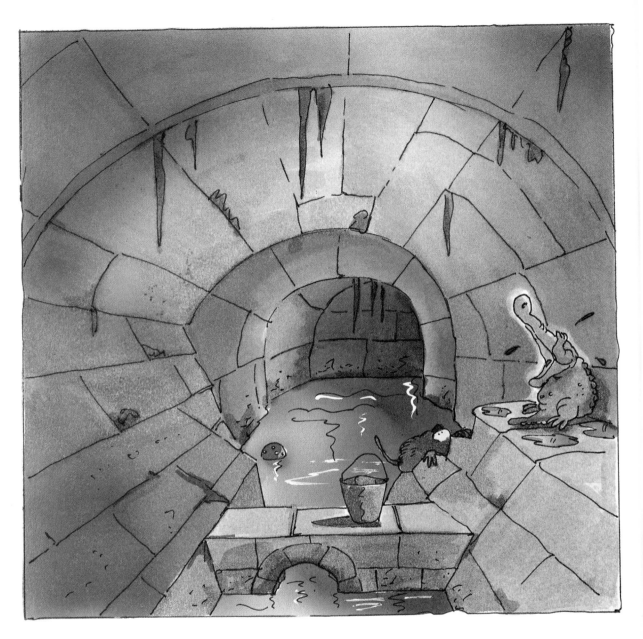

They both scrambled onto a little ledge, and Christabel began to cry — big crocodile tears.
"I want my Mummy, I want my Daddy, I want to go home," she wailed.

"Stop it — you'll cause another flood," said René.
Then he had a wonderful idea. "Let's find my Mum. She knows everything. She'll help you find your Mum and Dad."
He gave Christabel a big, snowy-white hankie.
"I wonder how he keeps it so clean?" she thought.

Then René had another wonderful idea.
"If I ride on your back, we can go ever so fast and I'll be able to see better," he said.
Off they went.
"Yippee! This is great! I always wanted to be a cowboy."

On and on went the tunnel .... and Christabel .... and
René .... until they turned a corner and ....

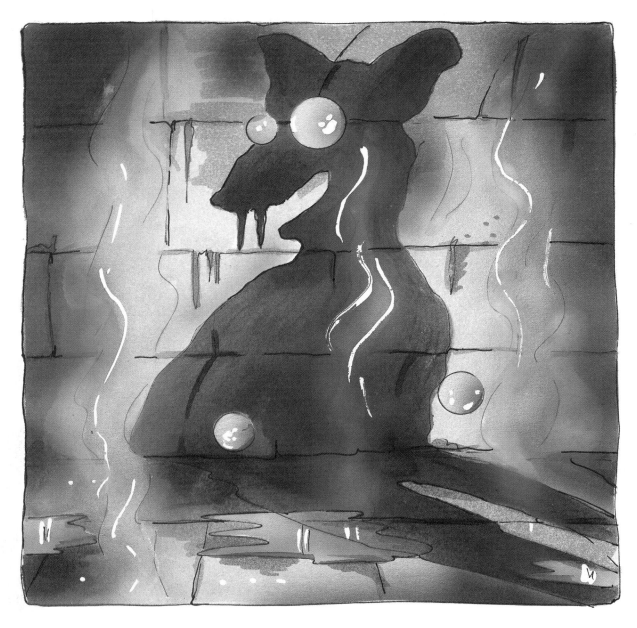

"Aaargh! There's a monster behind you," yelled Christabel. Christabel and René clutched each other in panic. They watched the enormous shadow on the wall grow larger and larger.

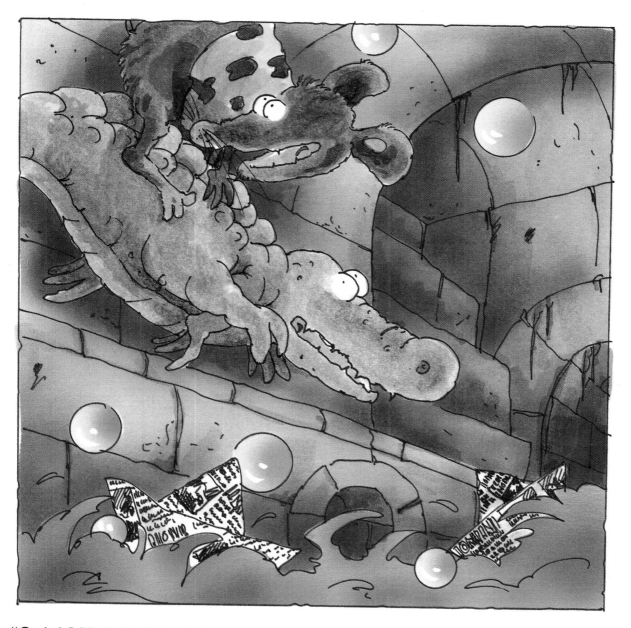

"Quick! Hide behind that pipe," said René, diving for cover and dragging Christabel with him.
They were only just in time. The towering monster's footsteps were getting very close.

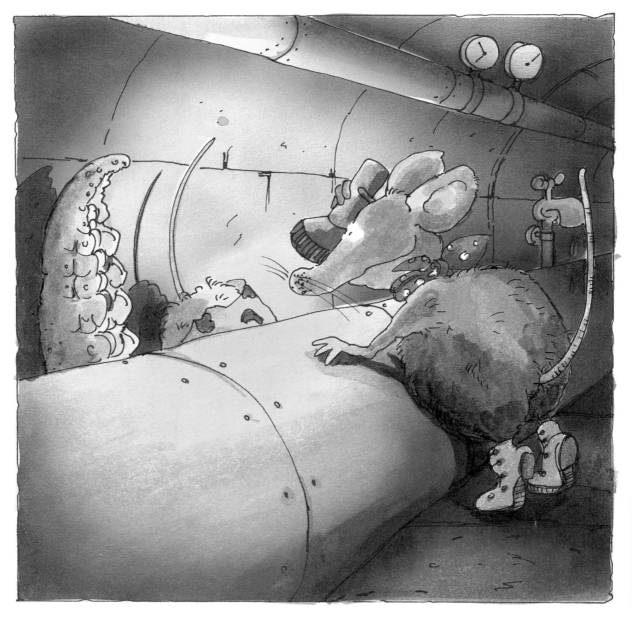

"Come out of there, René — and bring your friend," said Mrs Rat.
"Mum," said René, faintly.

René explained all about Christabel.
"Don't you worry, dear," said Mrs Rat, "I've been running round these sewers all my life. We'll have you out of here in no time."
"I told you my Mum would solve everything," whispered René to Christabel.

"Lots of steps now children, so be careful. You can count them —
there are 177."
"15, 16, 17," said Christabel.
"19, 20, 21," said René.
"I think you missed a number out," said Mrs Rat.

At the top of the 177 stairs were some rungs, and at the top of the rungs — blue sky.
Christabel thought she could hear her Daddy snoring.
"I can't climb those," she wailed.

Mrs Rat thought and thought.
"We could try that old tunnel we made to Auntie Flo's in the Rodent House … Hmm, we might have to make it a bit bigger."

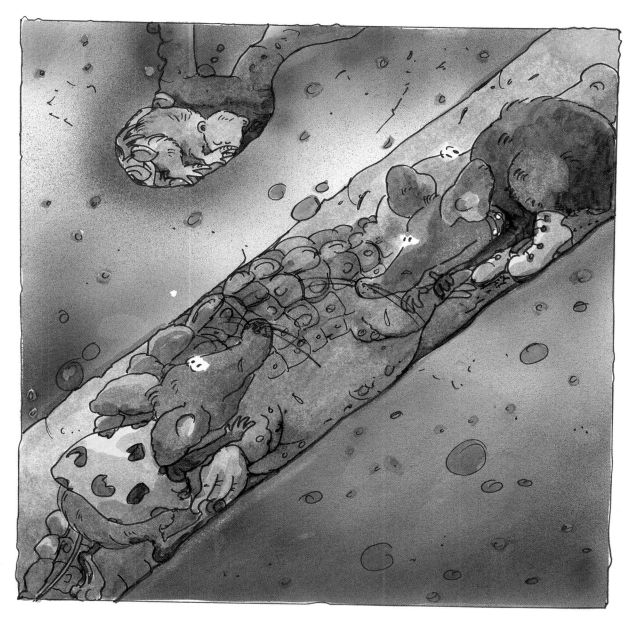

Mrs Rat and René started to push Christabel slowly along the tunnel. Christabel tried to help by not breathing too much. It was a tight squeeze.

"Just a little further and you are out," puffed Mrs Rat.
"Quietly, and you might get away with it," giggled René.
"I hope your Mum and Dad haven't been worrying about you,"
said Mrs Rat.

"You have a special door now," said Mrs Rat, "so you must come and see us next Sunday. Tell me what crocodiles like to eat and I'll make you a special treat."

"You have been a good girl, Christabel," said Mrs Crocodile,
"you haven't made a sound all morning."
"I've had such a nice nap, too," yawned Mr Crocodile, "and now I'm
ready for a swim. Oh good, they're just refilling the pool now.
I wonder who pulled the plug out?"